The Life and Death of a Brave Bull

The Life and Death of a Brave Bull

BY MAIA WOJCIECHOWSKA

WITH DRAWINGS BY JOHN GROTH

HARCOURT BRACE JOVANOVICH, INC., NEW YORK

ISBN 0-15-245200-1

Library of Congress Catalog Card Number: 77-181537

Printed in the United States of America

First edition

B C D E F G H I J

The author and the publisher thank Luis de Ascasubi for permission to
reprint a passage from his book *Of Bulls and Men*; and Charles Scribner's
Sons for permission to include a quotation from *Death in the Afternoon*
by Ernest Hemingway, Copyright 1932 Charles Scribner's Sons; renewal
copyright © 1960 Ernest Hemingway.

For Gregory Hemingway

"To see two bulls fight is a beautiful sight. They use their horns as a fencer does his weapon. They strike, parry, feint, block, and have an exactitude of aim that is amazing. When they both know how to use the horn the combat usually ends as does a fight between two really skillful boxers, with all dangerous blows stopped, without bloodshed and with mutual respect. They do not have to kill each other for a decision."

—*Death in the Afternoon* by Ernest Hemingway

"One of the most beautiful sights that the animal kingdom can offer is the fullgrown, majestic, fighting bull in action. Its unending bravery, its pride, one might even say its Spanish haughtiness, were the very qualities expected of the Spanish knights. The spirit of the *Conquistadores* is ever present in the *toro de lidia* and it is no wonder that the fighting bull took on a totemic character. The knights of old fought and died for their faith, their King, their ladies, or their honor, and the bulls fought and died as they did because they had been bred by these same knights." —*Of Bulls and Men* by Don Luis de Ascasubi

His death was decided
before his birth.

"I want a bull that will make bullfighting history for me as he dies," said a bullfighter who had just been declared *El Número Uno,* the best killer of bulls in Spain that year.

"I shall let you choose the bull and the cow that will give life to the animal that will make bull-fighting history for you," said the breeder of bulls to the bullfighter.

The cow that the bullfighter chose
during the testing for bravery
came to the pic six times.
Drained of strength,
and knowing that the pic
was the origin of pain,
she still would have come back to it
again and again.

"I shall further test this cow," said the bullfighter. "I shall fight her now."

She charged straight
two dozen times, and
there was no treachery
nor cunning
nor fear
in her attacks.

"Now to find a strong bull worthy of that brave cow," said the one who that year was the Number One bullfighter in all of Spain. Although the breeder prided himself on having only animals who came from a long line known for their nobility and courage, the bullfighter rejected twelve before he saw the one worthy of the cow.

He charged the horse three times
before his great horns
lifted the horse, together with the rider,
and spun both around,
tossing the
great living weight
against the wooden fence.
A hand clapped against the wooden door,
attracting his attention.
He left the testing ring
not at a trot,
but slowly, majestically,
proud of his own strength.

"When the one he fathers is six," *El Número Uno* said, "I shall kill him in Madrid, and his death shall be greater than the lives of those who gave him birth."

He was born with a bellow
so loud that he frightened
his mother who had never known fear.

During the first year of his life
he had but two needs:
eating and resting.

And he never went wanting for either.
His world was a sea of grass,
wide and endless;
green during the day,
black at night.

Before he turned two,
he discovered himself
the owner of a wondrous toy—
his horns.
They were not fully grown yet,
but they curved inward
and ended with the sharpness of knives.

With his horns,
he would now attack
anything
that moved
into the path of his perfect vision.

At first
shadows of passing clouds,
a wind-blown leaf,
the moving grass,
a rock, a tree trunk
were his targets.
But soon he began to use
his horns
as weapons
against other bulls.

He stood no chance with the older ones,
but with the young, he fenced well.
The steers, by their very presence,
would calm his desire to fight.
But he also loved to run.
His swift legs
he used against the men on horseback
who invaded his domain.

And they came often,
their long lances
upsetting his balance,
sending him sprawling across the green
   grass.
But no matter how fast he ran,
and no matter how hard he tried to reach
the horses' flanks,
he could never touch them,
for the horses were faster than he
and the men's lances kept him away
from their glistening flesh.

He was totally different from the steers.
There was something mysterious and
  wondrous
in his blood,
which made him happiest when
he fought other bulls
or gave chase
to the mounted men.

But he was not different from other brave
  bulls.
The joy of the fight
and of the chase
was bred into
his blood.

At the end of his second year
he left his pasture for the first time.
A dozen men on horseback,
at first very small against the flat land,
then growing taller than he,
came to drive him and the other two-year-olds
away from where they lived and fought and
  grazed.
Together with the others
he gave chase across miles of green sea.
The black bulls of death,
kept together by steers,
chased after the men and their mounts.

But, by chasing them, the young bulls did
   not know
that they ran where the men wanted them to go.

Noon came and went,
and the sun disappeared
beyond the flatness of the land
by the time the chase had ended
inside a large pen.

There was no grass and no breeze inside the pen.
There were flies and heat and thirst.

The one who willed him to be born, the one they still called the best sword in Spain that year, was among those who saw him the next day, for he was to be tested as his mother and his father had been tested before him and as all two-year-olds were tested each year.

His testing ground
was a circular prison
of wood and sand,
a pic held by a man on a horse,
and men's eyes watching from the stands.
Separated from the others,
he waited his turn in a dark passageway.
When the gate opened
a hand waved in the light,
and he burst out
of the unfamiliar darkness
into the known brightness of a noonday sun.

His eyes took it all in at once:
the mounted horse,
the circle of sand,
the wooden fence,
the faces of men.
But his brain understood only one fact:
the horse and the man with the lance
were imprisoned with him
inside the circle of sand.

With a great snort of pride in his strength
and joy in the fact
that the man and the horse were trapped,
he attacked.

Before he could hit the horse
with his horns,
the tip of the pic
drove the sharpness of steel
into his lowered neck.
With all his two-year weight,
with all his joyous strength,

he pushed against the pain,
his mouth shut tight,
eyes open and fixed on his prey.
The more he pushed the pain,
the deeper the pain went.
The wetness on his back spread
and then fell red on the yellow sand.
Yet he did not leave the pic once
while its steel tip cut down on his wind
but not on his want
to hold the horse at bay,
to fight.

"A truly great bull!" said the bullfighter. "His bravery makes him ignore the pain."

He would have struggled all day and all
   night
against the horse, the pic, and the man,
against the taste of hurt,
against the temptation
that lurked in his weakened neck
to give in, give up.
His blood was stirred hot by the fight;
his sweat ran down his flanks,
mixing with the red blood of his wound;
his powerful body was eager for more.
And when they applauded him with cheers,
he did not hear.

A waved cape
tossed over the wooden fence
distracted his attention from the horse,
and he attacked the cape.

It disappeared before he
could drive his horns into it.
He turned around
to find
the man, the pic, and the horse
gone.
And he was all alone
in the circle of sand.

In his anger
he attacked the fence.

And his right horn,
the one he favored,
his toy,
his weapon,
broke,
hung blinding him for a second,
and then fell.
With the other horn
he attacked
what he had lost,
his right horn.

"He could have been the best of his breed," the rancher said. "But now he will never fight in a bullring. He will die of old age." "What a pity," someone whispered. And someone else laughed. "I wouldn't mind fighting him now myself." And the bullfighter felt some unknown, unexplained, personal dread. He who had chosen this bull to be born said not a word and turned his head away from the sight of the animal who, having nothing to fight, still fought his lost horn.

Back on the pasture,
the great wound in his back healed,
and flesh and hair covered the place
where once his right horn had grown.
He fought other bulls with
his one remaining horn.
It was hard to do—
it was like going into each battle
knowing that he would lose.
But his want to fight
was greater than that knowledge.

Often he would spend long nights
licking his wounds.
His body always ached,
and he would moan
in his sleep.

But he bore his wounds with pride
and fought more often than the rest
of the bulls, who had been born,
as he was,
with the want to fight in their blood.

And whenever the horsemen came,
he would give chase.
He was heavier but also faster and wiser now,
and sometimes he would graze the horses'
   flanks
with his only horn,
but more often they would get away from
   him,
and he would stand,
panting, his body heaving,
his mouth closed tight,
looking at them getting smaller
and disappearing finally against the endless
   sky.

When he was four,
some of the bulls that were born
at the same time as he
went away never to come back.
But he stayed.

By the time he was five
he had learned to manage
with his one horn so well
that most bulls
gave him a wide berth.
And those who fought him
would bow to his greater strength
and skill by moving away from him
at a trot after they'd fought.

When he was six,
the rest of the bulls born
at the same time as he
went away never to come back.
But he stayed—

with the cows,
the steers,
the seed bulls,
and the younger animals.

Food and rest
ceased to give him pleasure.
But the chase after horses
and the duels with other bulls
still made his blood hot
with his one great need.
And the need was to prove his strength,
to stretch his courage.

He grew old.

He had fathered more than a hundred bulls,

who at four or six were killed in various
   rings.

One of his sons killed the man

who that year in Spain

was called *El Número Uno*.

But he was not the same man

who had willed the old bull's birth.

That one no longer held the title.

He had always fought bulls for his own pleasure most of all. And his pleasures came from encountering bulls that stretched his own courage to the breaking point by their own lack of fear. When he had been the best sword in Spain, those were the only bulls he fought and killed. And he killed each with a great respect for death and joy over the fact that those animals were too noble for the butcher's knife.

When he was no longer considered the best, his art too private to please the crowd, the bravest bulls were denied him. And when that time came, he remembered the bravest of all the bulls, the one whose birth he had willed, the one who had lost a horn before he could be fought.

It was said that his art had become too private to please the crowds. But he himself blamed his decline on the decline of bravery in the bulls. And for his last fight, before he retired from the bullring, he wanted to challenge that particular one-horned bull, the one whose birth he had willed. His bravery and strength, he knew, would have increased with years, and he would have become too dangerous to fight. But what the bullfighter wanted for his last fight was to discover the furthest reaches of fear and the furthest boundaries of courage.

In the spring of his ninth year,
early one morning,
when the dew was bright like rain
on the fragile blades of grass,
they came for him.
A steer led him into a truck.
When the truck stopped, he was led out
into a pen.

It was different from the pen he remembered.
The smells were not the same,
and this time he did not mind the heat,
the flies, and the lack of grass.
The gate was larger this time,
and when it opened
there was a circle of sand, of wood,
and circle after circle
of men's faces in the stands.

It was five o'clock in the afternoon,
exactly five o'clock in the afternoon,
as he burst out from beyond the gate of fear.
His gigantic body
(for he weighed well over a ton)
made the earth tremble,
and they gasped
at his sheer size,
for not one of those who saw him
had ever seen
a nine-year-old in the ring before.
But then they saw that he was
missing a horn,
and the laughter was loud from the stands,
and the shouts were mocking from the stands.

But he heard neither the laughter
nor the shouts
because
for the very first time
in his life

his

target

was

a

standing

man.

He charged.

The bright magenta
of the flowing cape
remained on the side of his one horn
as he charged
and
charged
again,
the movement of the lure
satisfying his great want to attack.

And when the horses came,
and there were two this time,
imprisoned with him on the sand,
he charged one,
drove his horn into the padding.
As the pic tired his back,
he pushed until the horse and rider went
 down;
then he turned and rushed the other horse.

He took the *banderillas*
without tossing their sting away
and came,
with his great head lowered,
to the redness of the cloth
that hid the sword.

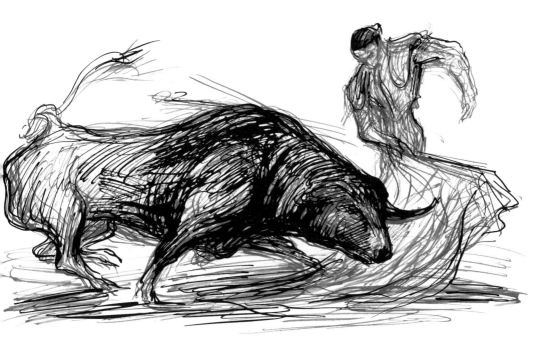

The people had stopped laughing long before, because the one who had once been Number One in the land was fighting the one-horned bull always on the side of the horn. And the man knew his trade well as he fought the bull that towered with courage and pride.

The sight of the black bull and the man, each giving his best, each living a lifetime during the twenty minutes on the yellow sand, was a sight that made good men cry.

He did not know that he fought more bravely
than any other bull that year in Spain.
He did not know that the man
in the ring with him
grew to love him for his courage,
for his great nobility,
for his immense strength
and his endless wish to attack.

He did not know that those
who had seen him,
who at the first sight of him had laughed,
now honored him
by giving him
three trips
around the ring,
his left toy, his weapon,
his only horn,
drawing three perfect circles
into the grains of sand,
while the people cheered.

By then he was quite dead.

And his death
was the death of
a brave bull.